Chapter 1
War

'There's going to be a war and the factory will have to close,' John Logie Baird told his apprentice in despair.

Fourteen-year-old Alex was pale and thin. If he lost his job there'd be no money for his widowed mother who was too ill to work. But Alex had heard on the wireless that nothing was going to stop war breaking out between Great Britain and Germany.

'Maybe television will come in useful in the war effort,' Alex suggested hesitantly.

But Baird shook his tousled head. He was a delicate-looking man, and had had a weak chest since boyhood. Sometimes Alex's thin figure reminded Baird of himself as a child. He knew they were alike in another way too – they both had a burning curiosity about how things worked.

'Enemy aircraft approaching Britain would be able to lock on to a target using a television beam,' he explained to Alex gloomily. 'That means we could be helping the German High Command to knock out London. We're finished.'

Pictures Through
the Air

The Story of John Logie Baird

Anthony Masters

Illustrated by Linda Clark

an imprint of Hodder Children's Books

John Logie Baird (1888-1946)

13 August 1888 John Logie Baird was born at Helensborough, near Glasgow.

1912 Baird gained a diploma in electrical engineering from the Royal Technical College, Glasgow.

1924 He transmitted the flickering image of a Maltese Cross over a distance of a few feet.

26 January 1926 Now living in London, Baird gave the world's first demonstration of television in his attic before an audience of about fifty scientists. In the same year he demonstrated Noctovision.

1927 Baird transmitted television over 438 miles of telephone line between London and Glasgow.

1928 Television was transmitted across the Atlantic, from London to New York, for the first time.

1929 The BBC started broadcasting a television service, using the Baird system.

1930 Baird demonstrated big screen television at the London Coliseum.

1931 The Derby was transmitted by Baird on to a large cinema screen in London.

1937 Baird's television transmission system was dropped by the BBC in favour of EMI's system.

1939 Baird's factory closed at the outbreak of the Second World War.

14 June 1946 Baird died at Bexhill, on the south coast of England.

Baird was right. With the outbreak of war in 1939, all BBC television programmes were stopped by the government and the Baird Television Company was closed down.

'I'm sorry.' Baird was close to tears as he spoke to his five hundred members of staff. 'We *did* have a future.'

'Will I ever see you again, sir?' Alex was desperate.

'Why not tomorrow?' asked Baird. 'I've got enough money to keep a few workers on.' He gazed at his apprentice steadily. 'I value you, Alex.'

The boy felt a surge of pride.

A few weeks later, Alex found Baird bent double in pain. He was in his forties now and his weak chest was getting worse.

'You need a holiday, sir. Why don't you go down to Cornwall? Isn't that where your wife and children have been evacuated?'

'I'll go on one condition,' said Baird. 'I'd like you to come with me. You need some sea air too.'

'I can't, sir. I've got Mum to look after.'

'Maybe she'll accept an old friend of mine dropping in to keep an eye on her,' said Baird. 'And I'll give her some of your wages in advance.'

Chapter 2
An Exciting Journey

When he boarded the train Alex was feeling shy. What on earth was he going to say to a famous inventor like John Logie Baird for such a long time?

But he needn't have worried. Baird wanted to talk.

'I got interested in electricity when I was your age,' he said as the train pulled out in a cloud of steam. 'I even created a home-made generator to supply the household, but the lights failed and Dad fell down the stairs. He still sent me to college though.'

Baird stared through Alex as if he was actually seeing the past. Then he went on, 'I was medically unfit for the army, so I got a job at the Clyde Valley Electrical Power Company. But because of my health I had to resign. I hated the job anyway…

'I'm a loner, Alex,' confessed Baird as the train rattled west.

He gazed through the window at the
rows of soot-blackened houses, while Alex
got out his picnic.

'My mum does these fantastic Spam
sandwiches, sir.'

Baird selected one and took an enormous
bite. 'This is delicious,' he said.

'How did you start inventing?' asked
Alex, hoping Baird wasn't going to eat too
much of his picnic. He didn't seem to have
brought any sandwiches of his own.

'I invented damp-proof undersocks. They were a great success. Then I went to Trinidad to make jam, and later a new kind of soap called Speedy Cleaner.'

Alex gazed at him in amazement as the train clattered out of the suburbs into the countryside.

'But I got so bored I decided to put Nipkow's theory to the test and see if I could transmit some television images instead.'

'What was Nipkow's theory?' asked Alex.

Baird leaned back in his seat and closed his eyes. 'Dr Nipkow was a Russian who made a rotating disc pierced with a spiral of square holes.'

He suddenly opened his eyes again and pulled out a pencil and a notebook from his jacket pocket. Resting the notebook on his lap, he began to draw the disc.

'Nipkow wanted to scan and then break up objects into light and dark elements. Those elements could be transmitted as electrical impulses to an identical disc rotating at a matching speed. The disc then converted the impulses back into pictures.'

Baird looked up at Alex eagerly as the train rocked over some points. 'Nipkow gave me the inspiration. Then I put my inspiration into practice.'

Chapter 3

Transmitting Bill

'How did you start?' asked Alex.

'I only had an attic as a workshop, but I managed to assemble this rather primitive first television set on a wash-stand.'

Just then, the ticket inspector arrived to check their tickets. Alex could hardly wait until he went away.

'I used an electric motor someone had thrown away,' Baird continued, 'rotating discs made from a hat-box, a darning needle, a projection lamp in a biscuit tin, lenses from a bicycle lamp and an awful lot of batteries. The set was held together by string and sealing wax.'

'Did it work?' asked Alex as the train roared into a tunnel.

When they came out, Baird was red in the face with delight.

'I transmitted the image of the Maltese Cross over a distance of 10 feet in a public hall in 1924. How about that?'

'Brilliant,' replied Alex.

'I'm not so sure,' said Baird with painful honesty. 'The Cross was flickering like mad, but at least I'd made a start.'

Baird got up from his seat, dragged
down his briefcase from the luggage rack
and pulled out a photograph of the Maltese
Cross transmission which was certainly very
blurred.

Alex looked at it eagerly, fascinated to
see this early example of Baird's work.

'Then I managed to transmit Bill.'

'Bill?' asked Alex in bewilderment.

'He was an old ventriloquist's dummy no one wanted,' said Baird.

'I put the dummy in front of the transmitter disc and his picture was received in the other room. It was 2 October 1925. I'll never forget that day. I was so delighted that I ran downstairs to the office below and persuaded an office boy to help with the experiment. He became the first living image to be transmitted by television.'

Baird smiled at Alex. 'I've got Bill in a cupboard at the factory. You two ought to meet. He's already famous. But you could be famous too one day, Alex. Who knows what kind of advanced television you might invent when I'm dead and gone?'

Baird began to cough, and Alex felt a moment of panic.

'I'd need to go to university,' he began.

Baird stopped coughing. 'Leave it to me,' he said, and Alex felt a thrill of excitement.

Chapter 4
Going Wrong

A girl, sitting with her mother by the window, gazed curiously at the rather sickly-looking man who hadn't stopped talking for a moment.

'The following year I invented Noctovision,' Baird was saying. 'And that was a forerunner to radar. Infra-red and ultra-violet rays can't be seen by us, but a television receiver is sensitive to them.'

The girl was amazed to see how intently the young boy was listening. She couldn't understand a word the man was saying.

'I placed an object in the dark, bathed in infra-red light,' Baird said. 'The light was then sent to a receiving set which turned electrical impulses back to light which would be visible to the human eye.'

'When did you start your television company?' Alex asked as the train began to slow down.

'In 1927,' replied Baird. 'And the following year we made the first trans-Atlantic television transmission between London and New York. We also transmitted to a ship in mid-Atlantic, and later we used colour as well as black and white.'

Alex saw that Baird was sweating and looking drained.

'Do you want to take a nap, sir?'

'Don't you mean you're getting bored?' asked Baird, and Alex couldn't work out whether he was teasing him or not.

But he had no time to find out. For, as the train picked up speed, Baird was off again. This time he was describing how he had built his first television receiving set in 1928.

'We carried out midnight transmissions from the roof of a building in London with a range of 5 miles. Then, in 1929, the BBC started an experimental television service using my system. The service started with sound and vision being transmitted separately, but by 1930 they were being broadcast together. The images were low-definition pictures on a 30-line system.'

'Why are the lines so important?' asked Alex.

'The more lines there are, the clearer the picture,' explained Baird.

Then Alex remembered an extraordinary event his mother had told him about.

'Didn't you once televise a horse race – the Derby I think it was, sir?' he asked.

'That's right,' smiled Baird. 'I set up a transmitter by the winning post. It was the first outside live broadcast and signals had to be sent down the telephone to be amplified in our London laboratory for transmission by the BBC. Anything could have gone wrong. But it didn't.

'Then things *did* start to go wrong,' said Baird, closing his eyes again. 'Horribly wrong.'

Another passenger, an old man sitting opposite, leaned forward anxiously.

'Is the gentleman feeling faint?' he asked Alex. 'I could open the window.'

'Then I won't hear what he's saying,' protested Alex. 'He's just a bit worked up, that's all.'

The old man shrugged and went back to his newspaper.

'I suggested there should be a competition for the best television service,' Baird continued. 'Well, everyone knows how badly the competition went wrong – for us! We just didn't have the money to produce the best system. So I began experimenting with cathode ray tube reception, where a beam of electrons passes through a tube filled with fluorescent gas. It forms an image where the beam strikes a screen at the far end.'

As Baird finished speaking, the old man put down his newspaper again and exclaimed, 'Am I in the presence of John Logie Baird, the inventor of television?'

'I wouldn't go as far as that,' began Baird, as Alex almost burst with pride.

'But I visited the London Coliseum to see your big screen television,' the man insisted. 'It was absolutely extraordinary.'

Baird continued impatiently. 'I wanted to set up a chain of cinemas that would use television receivers, and by 1936 my factory was well-known. My television receivers were regarded as the best on the market you know.'

The old man nodded, impressed.

As Baird and Alex got out at Penzance Station, two small children ran up.

'Malcolm and Diana – meet my apprentice, Alex.'

Then a woman arrived and threw her arms round Baird.

'And this is my wife, Margaret.'

She turned to Alex and asked, 'Did he let you get a word in on the journey?'

'Oh yes,' said Alex. 'Several, in fact.'

Chapter 5
No Time for Bombs

In 1940, soon after Baird and Alex arrived back in London, the Baird Television Company went bankrupt. All Baird had left now was his house, in which he set up a laboratory to research electronic colour television. He still had just enough money to employ a part-time assistant. He chose Alex, who worked in an armaments factory during the day and for Baird in the evenings and at weekends.

Sirens continually wailed, many
buildings were blackened ruins and there
were bomb craters in the roads. Some
people had shelters in their houses and
others slept in the tunnels of the London
Underground. But Baird never sheltered
anywhere.

One evening, during a severe air raid, Baird as usual refused to take cover.

As Alex made tea for them both, he couldn't find any milk or sugar.

'You'll have to do without,' snapped Baird. 'I've mislaid my ration book.'

'You've also forgotten to fix the blackout in the kitchen,' yelled Alex. 'We could be a target for a direct hit.'

A few days later, Alex heard the whistling of a bomb. The dreadful sound seemed to go on for ever until the bomb eventually fell, shattering part of Baird's roof.

Debris rained down and Alex was cut by flying glass.

'I'll just get some cotton wool,' he said, the blood streaming down his face.

'What do you want cotton wool for?' demanded Baird.

'To mop up some of this blood,' said Alex indignantly.

'Hurry up then,' shouted Baird. 'We haven't got all night.'

Oblivious to the wailing sirens and whistling bombs, Baird devoted himself to still more research. He invented a 600-line three-dimensional system and at least three types of electronic 500-line three-dimensional set.

Alex had failed his medical when he'd been called up for the army, just as Baird had before him. As a result, he was able to go on working for him.

In 1944, a few days after Alex's nine-teenth birthday, Baird invited the press to a demonstration of his recently patented Telechrome, the world's first all electronic colour and three-dimensional receiver. But the next day there was hardly any mention of the new invention in the newspapers.

'What's the matter with them?' demanded Baird.

'I don't think you've noticed. There's a war on, sir,' replied Alex.

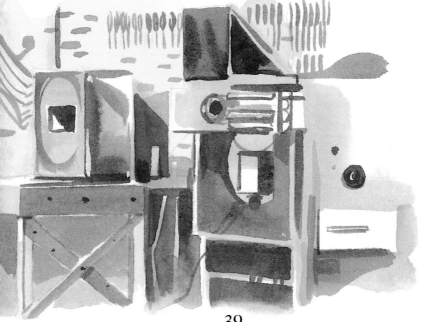

Chapter 6
Time and Tide

With his wife and children still in Cornwall, Baird felt isolated and ignored. Yet another bomb had damaged his house and the inventor was forced to live in cheap hotels.

'I can't afford to pay you any longer,' he finally told Alex.

'That doesn't matter, sir.'

'Of course it matters.'

'But I'm learning so much,' Alex pleaded, and Baird sighed.

'You're very loyal, Alex,' he said.

'I just see myself as lucky, sir.'

Alex continued to help Baird research colour, stereoscopic and big-screen experimental receivers. But, even though he was at last winning awards, Baird's health began to worsen.

The war ended in 1945 and in June 1946 the BBC announced the re-launch of television.

Baird was overjoyed, but he also doubted if there was any future for him in the industry.

'Most of it's your work anyway,' Alex told him.

Gradually, Baird became more optimistic, confident that his new Super Set would be able to receive BBC programmes with the most amazing clarity and brightness.

Journalists were invited to watch the victory parades on the new set. But on the day of the demonstration, Baird was taken ill.

'Do the demonstration for me, Alex,' he pleaded.

'Of course I will.'

'And there's something else.'

Alex gazed at Baird's pallor and the cold sweat on his brow.

'What is it, sir?'

'I've let you down. I hoped to give you a cheque so you could go to university after the war.'

'Don't worry about that,' said Alex firmly. 'I'm going. I'll find the money – it's the least I can do after all you've taught me.'

The journalists were impressed by the
demonstration of the Super Set, but Baird's
ill-health had finally caught up with him.

Alex was deeply shocked to receive a
telegram from Baird's wife:

'JOHN LOGIE BAIRD DIED 14 JUNE 1946.'

Grief-stricken, Alex returned to the empty factory. Baird would have been furious. Death had come too soon. He was only fifty-eight and his Super Set had never been marketed.

As Alex stood at the gates of the factory, he heard Baird's voice.

'Don't give up, Alex. You've got to be ambitious. You've got to go to university.'

'Don't worry, sir,' he muttered. 'I told you, I'll get there somehow.'

Glossary

amplify (in television) to make the field of vision bigger

cathode ray tube a device which projects a narrow beam of electrons on to a screen

electrical impulses waves of electricity

electrons minute particles charged with electricity

infra-red rays rays of light that are beyond the red end of the visible spectrum

live broadcast a programme that is broadcast as it happens

low-definition pictures pictures that are fuzzy and unclear

Maltese Cross a badge in the shape of a cross, used by the Knights of Malta

Noctovision transmission from a dark room using infra-red rays

scan to pass a beam over every part of the image in turn

stereoscopic in which two images are brought together to form a complete picture

ultra-violet rays rays of light that are beyond the violet end of the visible spectrum

wireless radio